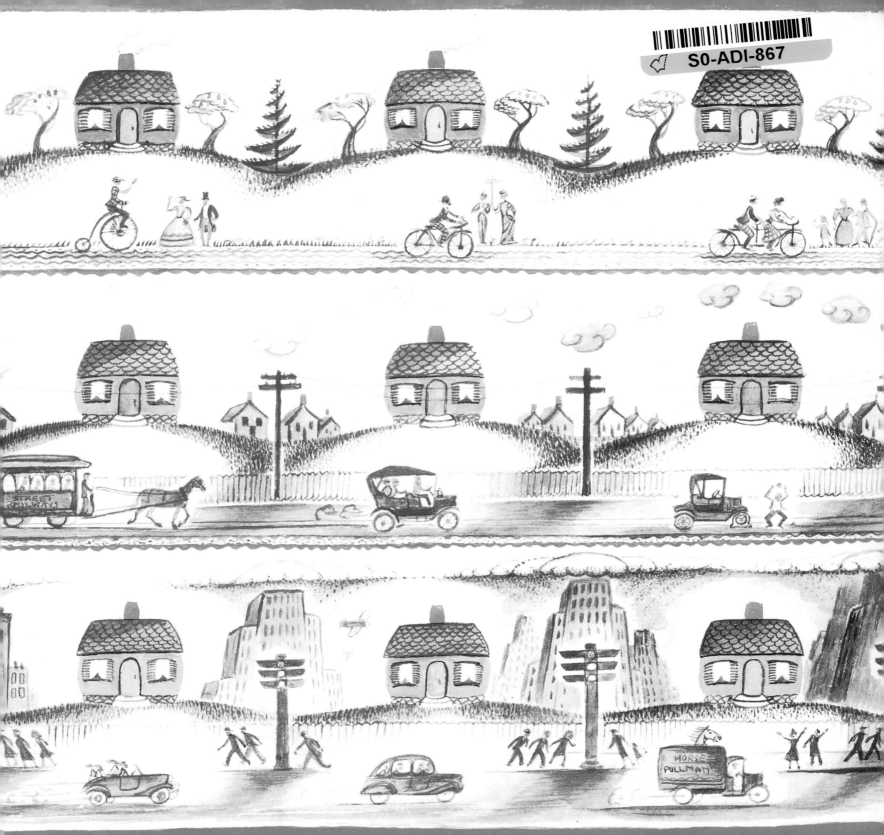

THE LITTLE HOUSE

STORY AND PICTURES
BY
VIRGINIA LEE BURTON

Houghton Mifflin Harcourt
Boston   New York

To Dorgie

The Library of Congress Cataloging-in-Publication data is on file.

ISBN: 978-1-328-74194-3 75th Anniversary edition
ISBN: 978-0-547-79044-2 Anniversary edition
ISBN: 978-0-395-25938-2 paperback
ISBN: 978-0-547-13104-7 board book

Manufactured in China
SCP 10 9 8 7 6 5 4

4500754146

Once upon a time
there was a Little House
way out in the country.
She was a pretty Little House
and she was strong and well built.
The man who built her so well said,
"This Little House shall never be sold
for gold or silver and she will live to see
our great-great-grandchildren's
great-great-grandchildren living in her."

1

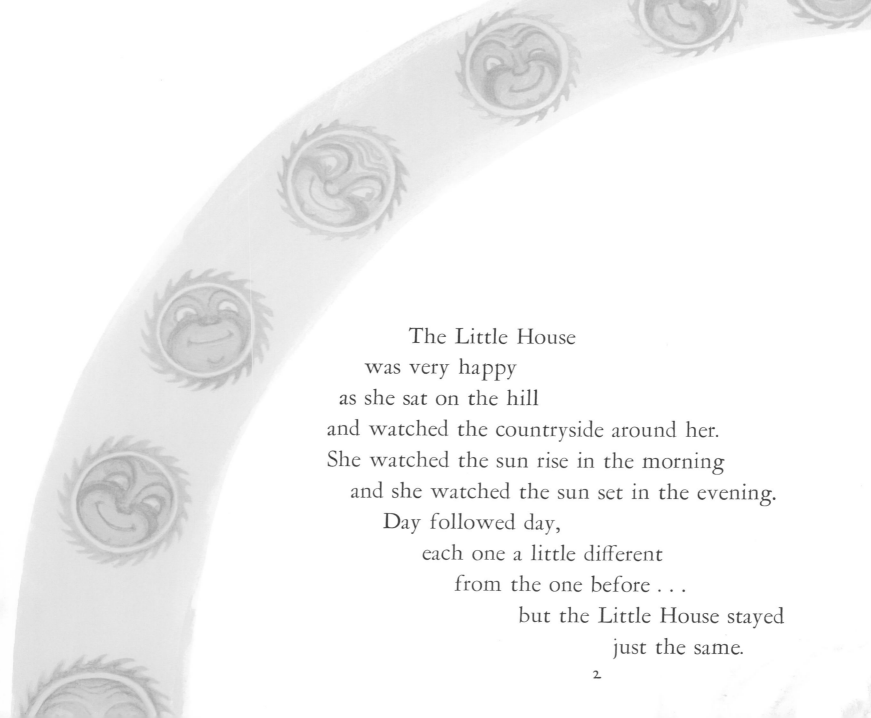

The Little House
was very happy
as she sat on the hill
and watched the countryside around her.
She watched the sun rise in the morning
and she watched the sun set in the evening.
Day followed day,
each one a little different
from the one before . . .
but the Little House stayed
just the same.

2

In the nights
she watched the moon grow
from a thin new moon to a full moon,
then back again to a thin old moon;
and when there was no moon
she watched the stars.
Way off in the distance
she could see the lights of the city.
The Little House was curious about the city
and wondered what it would be like to live there.

4

Time passed quickly
for the Little House
as she watched the countryside
slowly change with the seasons.
In the Spring,
when the days grew longer
and the sun warmer,
she waited for the first robin
to return from the South.
She watched the grass turn green.
She watched the buds on the trees swell
and the apple trees burst into blossom.
She watched the children
playing in the brook.

6

In the long Summer days
she sat in the sun
and watched the trees
cover themselves with leaves
and the white daisies cover the hill.
She watched the gardens grow,
and she watched the apples turn red and ripen.
She watched the children swimming in the pool.

8

In the Fall,
when the days grew shorter
and the nights colder,
she watched the first frost
turn the leaves to bright yellow
and orange and red.
She watched the harvest gathered
and the apples picked.
She watched the children
going back to school.

10

In the Winter,
   when the nights were long and the days short,
  and the countryside covered with snow,
she watched the children
coasting and skating.
  Year followed year. . . .
    The apple trees grew old
     and new ones were planted.
      The children grew up
       and went away to the city . . .
        and now at night
         the lights of the city
          seemed brighter and closer.

12

One day
the Little House
was surprised to see
a horseless carriage coming down
the winding country road. . . .
Pretty soon there were more of them
on the road and fewer carriages pulled by horses.
Pretty soon along came some surveyors and surveyed a line
in front of the Little House.
Pretty soon along came a steam shovel and dug a road
through the hill covered with daisies. . . .
Then some trucks came and dumped big stones on the road,
then some trucks with little stones,
then some trucks with tar and sand,
and finally a steam roller came
and rolled it all smooth,
and the road was done.

14

ROAD
CLOSED
FOR REPAIR
DETOUR

Now the Little House
watched the trucks and automobiles
going back and forth to the city.
Gasoline stations . . .
roadside stands . . .
and small houses
followed the new road.
Everyone and everything
moved much faster now than before.

16

More roads were made,
and the countryside was divided into lots.
More houses and bigger houses . . .
apartment houses and tenement houses . . .
schools . . . stores . . . and garages
spread over the land
and crowded around the Little House.
No one wanted to live in her
and take care of her any more.
She couldn't be sold for gold or silver,
so she just stayed there and watched.

18

Now it was not so quiet and peaceful at night.
Now the lights of the city were bright and very close,
and the street lights shone all night.
"This must be living in the city,"
thought the Little House,
and didn't know whether she liked it or not.
She missed the field of daisies
and the apple trees dancing in the moonlight.

20

Pretty soon
there were trolley cars
going back and forth
in front of the Little House.
They went back and forth
all day and part of the night.
Everyone seemed to be very busy
and everyone seemed to be in a hurry.

22

Pretty soon there was an elevated train
going back and forth above the Little House.
The air was filled with dust and smoke,
and the noise was so loud
that it shook the Little House.
Now she couldn't tell when Spring came,
or Summer or Fall, or Winter.
It all seemed about the same.

24

Pretty soon
there was a subway
going back and forth
underneath the Little House.
She couldn't see it,
but she could feel and hear it.
People were moving faster and faster.
No one noticed the Little House any more.
They hurried by without a glance.

26

Pretty soon they tore down
the apartment houses and tenement houses
around the Little House
and started digging big cellars . . . one on each side.
The steam shovels dug down three stories on one side
and four stories on the other side.
Pretty soon they started building up . . .
They built up twenty-five stories on one side
and thirty-five stories on the other.

28

Now the Little House only saw the sun at noon,
and didn't see the moon or stars at night at all
because the lights of the city were too bright.
She didn't like living in the city.
At night she used to dream of the country
and the field of daisies
and the apple trees
dancing in the moonlight.

30

The Little House
was very sad and lonely.
Her paint was cracked and dirty . . .
Her windows were broken and her shutters hung crookedly.
She looked shabby . . . though she was just as good a house as ever underneath.

Then one fine morning in Spring
along came the great-great-granddaughter
of the man who built the Little House so well.
She saw the shabby Little House, but she didn't hurry by.
There was something about the Little House
that made her stop and look again.
She said to her husband,
"That Little House looks just like the Little House
my grandmother lived in when she was a little girl,
only *that* Little House was way out in the country
on a hill covered with daisies
and apple trees growing around."

They found out it was the very same house,
so they went to the Movers to see
if the Little House could be moved.
The Movers looked the Little House all over
and said, "Sure, this house is as good as ever.
She's built so well we could move her anywhere."
So they jacked up the Little House
and put her on wheels.
Traffic was held up for hours
as they slowly moved her
out of the city.

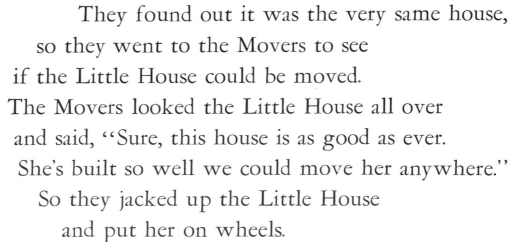

At first
the Little House
was frightened,
but after she got used to it
she rather liked it.
They rolled along the big road,
and they rolled along the little roads,
until they were way out in the country.
When the Little House saw the green grass
and heard the birds singing, she didn't feel sad any more.
They went along and along, but they couldn't seem to find
just the right place.
They tried the Little House here,
and they tried her there.
Finally they saw a little hill
in the middle of a field . . .
and apple trees growing around.
"There," said the great-great-granddaughter,
"that's just the place."
"Yes, it is," said the Little House to herself.
A cellar was dug on top of the hill
and slowly they moved the house
from the road to the hill.

The windows and shutters were fixed
and once again they painted her
a lovely shade of pink.
As the Little House settled down
on her new foundation,
she smiled happily.
Once again she could watch
the sun and moon and stars.
Once again she could watch
Spring and Summer
and Fall and Winter
come and go.

38

Once again
she was lived in
and taken care of.

39

Never again would she be curious about the city . . .
Never again would she want to live there . . .
The stars twinkled above her . . .
A new moon was coming up . . .
It was Spring . . .
and all was quiet and peaceful in the country.

When I was a young boy, my brother, Michael, and I moved with our parents, Virginia Lee Burton and the sculptor George Demetrios, into a house very much like the one pictured in this book. Like the little house in the book, our own little house and barn stood atop a hill, and had "a field of daisies with apple trees growing around." To us, it was an idyllic and magical setting, replete with a roaring brook, rocks to climb, and winding paths. My mother took the barn as her studio, and filled it with all manner of paraphernalia, and decades' worth of rubbish, that was eventually discarded so that the barn could truly become a working artist's studio. The barn was stripped down to its bare beams, and the spaces were filled with white panels, where eventually illustrations would hang and wallpaper the walls. My mother also kept many points of reference here in her barn-turned-studio. For instance, a few dull swords leaned in the corner—my brother and I would point them to the sky, standing in as Little John and Robin Hood, as we posed for another one of my mother's classic tales, *The Song of Robin Hood.* My mother used these points of reference to make sure her work was accurate and lifelike. With her unwavering commitment to excellence, and her vivid imagination and indefatigable energy, she would work from morning till night in that studio, ceaselessly researching and perfecting her craft.

At some point, when I was eleven or twelve, my mother went from being "Mommy" to "Jinnee"—a name that reiterated the many roles she played in her life. In all of them—ranging from mother to renowned author and illustrator, from teacher to designer, and from textile artist to comedian—she was a perfectionist. When you walked into the barn, the walls were always covered with illustrations—and very often, they were all drawings of the same page in the same book. This was a part of her process, as she was very much a visual thinker—something I inherited from her. She'd use these variations on an image as working drafts to see where she might have gone wrong, to try to go back and see how it might work differently. Impatient with herself, she'd hang all of the image iterations up to examine how she got from here to there—a documented path—which is how she thought about the book as the whole. Ironically enough, the book *The Little House* became our house, in a sense, as it was all-consuming, in the most positively best way, of course. Indeed, each year, my mother would draw our home as the cover of our Christmas cards for friends and family. And as she took artistic license in her drawings, so our actual home changed to coincide with her new renderings, in the way the wandering paths were carved, or the plants arranged, or the gardens designed.

When my brother and I were but rugrats, my mother would use us as research—her guinea pigs. In a sense, we were the precursors to the modern-day notion of a "focus group." She'd gather my brother and me and maybe two or three kids from the neighborhood and sit us down and read us the same story over and over for a month straight. If it kept our interest, then it was a good story. In her mind, it was essential to read a story aloud over and over again, and to think carefully about the words she used. In doing so, she tapped into the great oral tradition of storytelling, and found there a process that would work to insure that both her words and her illustrations resonated with our little souls, ensuring that her work would have a lasting legacy for children the world over. Jinnee's repeated efforts to make certain that the story and the illustrations became our favorite was part of her perfectionist approach—if we begged to have the story read to us over and over, she knew she was close to reaching her goal.

Among the many unique aspects of Jinnee's work is that if you look at the pages of *The Little House,* you'll notice that the house never moves on the page—it stays in one place and everything else moves around it. And trust me, this is not by accident. No word, no line, no element of design, no shape is out of place—it was all intentional, and that's what made her a truly groundbreaking genius. All of my mother's books have withstood the test of time, the test of generations of young readers, and no book has gone out of print. Her efforts to make every book a special treasure in the trove of every young reader is likely what accounts for their enduring legacy as among the greatest books of their time.

My mother gave us many gifts, but none so cherished as to have had the honor of being a part of her becoming an author who, seven decades later, is called the greatest author of children's books in the twentieth century. Nothing gives us more pleasure, and there is nothing of which we are prouder, than to hear a parent or a grand-parent or a child tell us that one of my mother's books was their very favorite book, and that night after night, they begged for it to be read to them. For these gifts, among others, we are eternally grateful to Jinnee for being a wonderful mother, and for the gift of being her sons.

—Aris Demetrios